THE
FIVE SISTERS

To Belinda – the best of creatures
MM

For John
PM

MARGARET MAHY

THE
FIVE SISTERS

Illustrated by
Patricia MacCarthy

VIKING

VIKING

Published by the Penguin Group
Penguin Books USA Inc., 375 Hudson Street, New York, New York 10014, USA
Penguin Books Ltd, 27 Wrights Lane, London w8 5tz, England
Penguin Books Australia Ltd, Ringwood, Victoria, Australia
Penguin Books Canada Ltd, 10 Alcorn Avenue, Toronto, Ontario, Canada m4v 3b2
Penguin Books (NZ) Ltd, 182–190 Wairau Road, Auckland 10, New Zealand

Penguin Books Ltd, Registered Offices: Harmondsworth, Middlesex, England

First published in Great Britain by Hamish Hamilton Ltd,
a division of Penguin Books Ltd, 1996
First published in the United States of America by Viking,
a division of Penguin Books USA Inc., 1997
A Vanessa Hamilton Book

1 3 5 7 9 10 8 6 4 2

Text copyright © Margaret Mahy, 1996
Illustrations copyright © Patricia MacCarthy, 1996
All rights reserved

isbn 0–670–87042–0
Printed in Great Britain
Filmset in 12 point Palatino

Contents

Chapter 1

Mysterious Voices

It was a soft, still summer day. Flowers hung their heads and dreamed of rain. Petals from the climbing rose fell softly into the lily pond. Sally, who had been drawing pictures, suddenly stopped scribbling and listened. All around her summer was sighing a great, slow, golden, secret sigh that only she could hear.

Her red felt pen seemed too slippery to hold properly. She let it fall, and it made a tiny rolling noise as it ran across the bricks. However, it was too hot for anyone, even a pen, to run far.

"Read to me, Nana?" Sally asked her grandmother, who was half-asleep in a green deck-chair.

"It's too hot to read," Nana murmured. "You *draw* for me instead. Draw me a nice, cool picture."

"It's too hot to *draw*," said Sally. "Just *tell* me a story."

Nana let her left hand drop sideways out of the deck-chair.

"Here I am," whispered a piece of white paper, slyly slipping itself between her fingers.

"Watch!" said Nana. She could not hear the paper's words, but she picked it up and folded it carefully.

"Here I go!" the paper hissed softly. "Changing! Changing!"

Nana's right hand reached out, searching for something. The red felt pen leapt eagerly between her twiddling fingers. As Sally watched over her shoulder, Nana began to draw on the folded paper.

"My turn at last!" said the red line sliding up and down the paper. "I'm so excited. What am I going to be?"

"I don't know," replied the red felt pen. "All you lines come out of me, but only the hand knows what you're going to turn into."

"I don't know either," said the hand. "I get instructions from above."

But neither Sally nor Nana could hear any of these mysterious voices on that hot, still, summer day.

Chapter 2

The Five Sisters

"It's a little girl," cried Sally. "A wild, adventurous girl with sticking-out ears."

The girl smiled back at Sally with a crooked smile. Her feet were wearing round, strong shoes, so it looked as if she could run all the way around the world. Her skirt, her hair and her red hair ribbon were all streaming to one side of her round face.

"She's blowing in the wind," said Sally, "even though there's no wind today."

"That wind is inside *me*," muttered the white paper. "I'm full of storms, stories and secrets. Write on me! Draw on me! Set them all free."

But Sally could not hear the voice of the paper.

"What's her name?" she asked Nana.

"Alpha," said Nana. "'Alpha' means 'first', and she's the first one."

"The first one of what?" asked Sally.

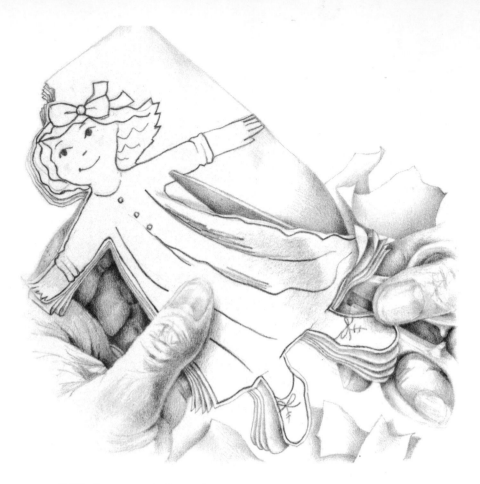

"I'll show you," said Nana.

She picked up the scissors and cut around Alpha's scarlet edges ("Changing! Changing!" the scissors and the paper whispered to one another.) Scraps fell to the ground. Nana unfolded Alpha; suddenly there were five girls in a row, all exactly the same shape, and all holding hands.

"What are the others called?" asked Sally.

"Oh, Sally, I'm *so* thirsty," Nana said. "Let's go inside and get some lemonade. Then we'll come back and think of names for them all."

"Lemonade with ice?" asked Sally.

"Of course," said Nana, folding Alpha and her four

sisters together again, and putting them on the edge of the lily pond. "It's definitely a day for ice."

"Back in a minute," Sally promised the five sisters. "Then we'll give you all names and faces."

But when Nana and Sally came back with their glasses of lemonade, cool and clinking with ice, the five sisters had quite disappeared. They were not on the edge of the pool. They were not floating among the rose petals. They could not have blown away because there was not a breath of wind down by the lily pond.

"Perhaps a fish stuck its head out and snapped them up," said Sally.

Nana shook her head.

"There aren't any fish left in my pool," she said. "Kingfishers have stolen them all."

Nana and Sally searched everywhere, but Alpha and her sisters were not to be found.

"Forget them," said Nana at last. "I'll cut out some more."

"But I want *those* sisters," said Sally. "They've run away to have adventures, and four of them don't have names, or even faces. How are they going to get on in the world without names or faces? I'll never forget them, Nana. I know I won't."

Chapter 3

A Dangerous World

While Nana and Sally were in the kitchen, sliding ice into their fizzing lemonade, Alpha, lying on the bricks beside the lily pond, had begun fizzing too. Her name sang a song inside her, and suddenly there she was – wide awake, and looking up through green leaves into blue sky. Immediately, a whole lot of words which had been hiding in the white paper rushed into her head.

"Where am I? What am I doing here?" Alpha asked the summer air.

"I don't know," said a beetle who was crawling across her. "One moment I was scrambling over mossy bricks, and then – bingo-bango! – *you* came tumbling out of the sky."

"Who am I?" Alpha asked again.

"Dunno," said the beetle in its rough voice, "but poor you, whoever you are! You've only got two legs, and that's just not enough to get along with."

"How many should I have?" asked Alpha.

"Six," said the beetle, crawling back on the bricks again. "Less than six is not enough, and more than six is far too many. Goodbye."

And he vanished, glad to be a beetle getting along on six legs.

"I'll try and sit up," thought Alpha and, because she tried very hard, and her four faceless, nameless sisters all pushed with her, she actually managed to curl herself upward. But this turned out to be dangerous. Alpha wasn't used to curling; it threw her off balance. Down she fell, into the lily pond.

"Hooray! It's a dangerous world!" she shouted. "But I'm glad it's not too safe to be interesting. Shall I shout for help? I don't think I can. I've been drawn too brave for that sort of shouting."

And none of the other sisters could shout for help, either. They had no mouths to shout with. The fifth sister, floating on the surface of the lily pond, held the others up out of the water as well as she could. Somehow, though she herself stayed dry, Alpha could feel wetness creeping through that fifth sister folded so neatly under her.

Up in the tree that grew by Nana's back door, a kingfisher looked down into the pool, hoping to see his afternoon tea swimming among the water lilies.

"Aha! A fish!" he thought, and he shot down to the pool. *Whizz! Snap!*

Off he flew, with the sisters clamped in his powerful beak, making for the hole in the bank where his chicks were waiting to be fed.

Chapter 4

The Island on the Edge of the Sea

Alpha felt warm summer air rushing over her. Her adventurous smile grew even wider.

"Wheee! This is fun," she cried.

The kingfisher was amazed.

"Fun?" he thought. "This fish must be mad. I don't want my chicks eating mad fish."

"Fly faster!" cried Alpha, smiling her adventurous smile, and squeezing the hand of the sister next to her.

The kingfisher was so alarmed at having a fish tell him what to do, and in such a happy voice, too, that he opened his beak in mid-air. The sisters fell free and began to drift down towards the treetops, unfolding as they fell. However, Alpha did not look down at the leaves below her. She looked *out*.

"I can see something wonderful!" she called, describing things for her sisters who had no eyes to see for themselves. "There is a great, big, blueness. That's the sky. And then there is *another* big blueness *under* the sky. I think it must be the sea. And far, far away, right on the edge of the sea, I think I can see an island. It's a little bit misty, but – yes – it really is an island.''

Just then a wandering breeze snatched up the sisters for a moment or two. It couldn't be bothered going down into the gardens below, but it enjoyed tossing and teasing them, and turning them over and over in the high summer air. They held hands tightly as they tumbled over the treetops, with Alpha leading the way. Though they had no eyes, her four sisters could some-how *feel* what Alpha was seeing. Treetop pictures flowed

down her arm and through her hand to the sister next to her, and *she* sent them on to the third sister who sent them to the fourth, who sent them to the fifth one, the wet one, the one who came last in the line.

"Wow! Exciting," Alpha cried. "Absoluto magnifico!"

The other sisters, though, did not really enjoy turning head over heels between the greenness of the trees and the blueness of the sky in quite the same way that Alpha did.

Then the breeze lost interest. It dropped them and flew away over the sea. But, just for a magical moment, the sisters hung, quivering in mid-air, held up by the secret sigh of the summer day.

"It *is* an island," Alpha cried. "I can see it clearly now. I can see a ruined city full of bears. I can see cowboys, aliens from another planet landing in their spaceship, and a gang of pirates burying treasure in the sand."

That was all she had time to see and say. Drifting and swaying, first one way and then the other, the sisters began floating down, down, down. Treetops rose up around them, hiding the sea and the island of adventure.

At last, they came to rest on short grass, shaggy with clover flowers. By now the fifth sister was drying out nicely, though what with the water, wind and sunshine she was starting to wrinkle slightly.

"I *loved* flying," said Alpha. "Let's fly again."

"Safe at last," thought the other four sisters, grateful to be resting on the grass surrounded by the lovely scent of clover.

But they were not safe. They were in terrible danger. A fearsome sound, half-way between a scream and a roar, burst into the sticking-out ears that Nana had drawn under Alpha's short red hair. She couldn't begin to guess what animal could make such a dreadful sound.

"Here it comes," cried a nearby clover plant. "Here comes the lawn-mower. Lie low, whatever you do."

"We're lying as flat as we can," replied Alpha. "Breeze! Breeze! Where are you?"

But the breeze was much too far away to hear her.

Chapter 5

Escape from the Shadow of a Tin Lip

The lawn-mower slid across the lawn, screaming as it came.

"I'll chase you, chip you, chop you, chew you,
Crunch you, munch you, scrunch you up!
I'll dice you, shred you, slice-like-bread you,
Crash you, smash you, slash you up."

The five sisters were sure that that was exactly what was going to happen to them.

"Breeze!" shouted Alpha again. "Breeze, where are you? We don't want to be chopped up by a lawn-mower. Rescue us! Breeze!"

Her words whirled into the air, dancing desperately like summer gnats, as the lawn-mower bore down on them.

"Got you!" it roared, and the advancing shadow of its tin lip fell over the sisters, lying hand in hand among the clover flowers.

But, just as that terrible, greedy shadow was about to slide across them, all five sisters were snatched up and away. Someone waved them about in the air.

"Paper dolls!" a boy's voice exclaimed in surprise. "Breeze," he called. "Here they are, Breeze! I've rescued them."

The boy's name was Eric and, by a funny coincidence, Breeze was the name of his big sister. She had been working on her art-folder for school the next day when she had heard her name called, over and over again, in a thin, far-away voice, no bigger than the voice of a dancing gnat. Breeze did not know whether or not to believe in it. Nevertheless, she had gone to the window and looked into the garden below. Her mother was mowing the lawn and there, in the very path of the lawn-mower, she had seen the sisters stretched out, hand in hand. So she had shouted to Eric, who had raced across the grass and snatched them up just in time. Then he carried them upstairs to the desk where Breeze was working.

"I wonder where they came from," Breeze said, folding and unfolding the sisters. "This first one's a bit scribbly, but I like her smile. And look! She has her hair ribbon on the *left*-hand side of her hair, but the second one has her hair ribbon on the *right*-hand side. The third one is the same as the first. She has a left-hand ribbon, but the fourth one has a right-hand ribbon. And the fifth one . . ."

"On the left!" said Eric. "They're like one another's reflections."

"Shall I paint faces and dresses for them all?" asked Breeze. "I think I will."

She spread the five sisters in front of her, and began

20

painting the second one. First of all she painted a blue dress. Then, while the blue paint dried, she painted brown hair, streaked it with yellow, as if it had been bleached by the sun, and tied it with a bright, purple hair ribbon. By the time she had finished painting the hair and the ribbon the dress was dry, so, choosing a very fine brush this time, Breeze stippled tiny purple and white flowers all over the blue. Then she painted black shoes and blue socks on the round feet, and at last, very carefully, she began to paint the face. Thin black eyebrows . . . bright blue eyes . . . red cheeks, and a red smiling mouth.

As Breeze painted she felt herself changing.

"What's happening to me?" she wondered. "I've always liked painting, but I am actually beginning to feel as if I want to paint pictures every day for the rest of my life. These sisters are putting a spell on me."

She put a tiny spot of white in each of the blue eyes, and suddenly the blue eyes sparkled and shone.

"There!" said Breeze, sitting back and looking, in a puzzled way, at the second sister.

"Hello," said a voice, but it was a voice that only Alpha could hear. "Are you there, Alpha? This is me, right next to you."

Alpha's heart leapt with joy when she heard one of her sisters actually say her name.

"It's a funny smile," said Eric, looking at the newly painted face. "She looks as if she knows a lot of secrets."

"Not secrets!" answered Breeze. "Stories. She's a story-teller."

"She's just been painted," said Eric. "How can *she* know any stories?"

Breeze knew the answer, but she did not know how she knew it.

"She's made of paper," she explained to Eric. "Paper has all the stories in the world hidden in it. Right now, all those stories are working their way into Cathabelle's head. That's her name, by the way, Cathabelle!"

"*I* told her what my name was!" Cathabelle murmured to Alpha. "They can't hear the voices of the world the way we do, but sometimes we can work our way into their thoughts and tell them what to say. I know a story about that. I think I know stories about many things."

"Paint the next one," suggested Eric, who was becoming more and more interested in the five sisters.

Breeze dipped her fine paintbrush in the black paint and painted two eyes with long eyelashes and elegant, arched eyebrows. But then she hesitated.

"I feel so strange," she said. "I feel as if I've changed from being one thing into being another. I'm going down into the garden to look around, and throw the Frisbee for the dog to chase. I'll finish the faces later." And she leaned the five sisters, hand in hand, against the books at one end of her bookcase. They were standing right behind a china pig, dressed in a clown's suit. He was holding a big book in one of his front trotters, and waving a white stick striped with gold in the other. He had green eyes with specks of darkness in them which were like sparkles turned inside out. Anyone with a head full of stories (anyone like Cathabelle, say) could easily recognize a wicked magician and, judging from that inside-out sparkle in his eyes, a magician who was not only wicked, but angry, as well.

Chapter 6

Off and Away!

As Breeze and Eric left the room, the pig spoke.

"Get out!" he growled. "This whole shelf is totally *mine*."

"No, it's not," said Cathabelle. "I can see seven tin owls on the other side of you. And then there's a ballet dancer standing on a blue box. And, after that, I can see a glass ball with a little garden in its heart, and *then* a black china cat with a black china kitten and –"

"Shut up! That's quite enough!" cried the pig, working himself into a fury. "I was the first one on this shelf. I took possession of it in the great and wonderful name of Magico-Porkus. Being jostled by stupid owls and ballet dancers is bad enough, but I'm not putting up with five paper sisters reading the spells in my book over my shoulder. I've had enough."

"*I* can't read over your shoulder," said Alpha. "My eyes are drawn so that they look to the right."

"And *I'm* looking to the left," said Cathabelle.

All the same, they both knew that Magico-Porkus's book really *was* open at a page of magical spells, and that someone really was reading it over his shoulder. But who?

"Don't worry! We're not staying," Alpha said, hoping to reassure the bad-tempered pig-magician. "We'll be off and away to have a few more adventures at any moment now."

"I said I have had enough!" shouted Magico-Porkus. "Beware of any magician who feels he's had enough. Where sensitive magicians are concerned, enough is the same as too much. So I am going to magic-up a bolt of lightning. It will strike in through the open window and – ZAP! – burn you to ashes."

"Then it will burn the bookcase too," Alpha pointed out.

"No, it won't," muttered the pig. "This will be a very tiny bolt of lightning. Just enough to burn up five silly sisters made of paper."

He began to grunt and chant and wave his gold-striped wand.

"Lightning! Lightning! Strike a blow!
Strike five sisters in a row.
Burn their ribbons! Burn their sashes!
Bring them all to dust and ashes."

"We don't have sashes," argued Alpha.

"OK! OK! But it has to rhyme," Magico-Porkus cried sulkily. "Engines drive cars, and rhymes drive spells."

Looking left, out into the garden, Alpha could just see a small, black cloud swelling up out of nothing, like a sinister balloon. It began drifting towards the open window, and, as it passed the plum tree, a flash of lightning, sharp and fierce as a needle, leapt out from it and struck a dry leaf, which flared and burnt to nothing in the blink of an eye. "We are going to burn too," thought Alpha sadly. "What a pity, when there's still so much to see and do."

Then a strange thing happened. Alpha's mind began to fill with words, and they weren't her own words. They came from somewhere outside her, flowing into her from Cathabelle. When Alpha spoke these words aloud, it felt as if she were speaking with someone else's

27

voice. It wasn't Cathabelle's, for Cathabelle was using her own voice to speak at exactly the same time as Alpha, and to say exactly the same thing.

> "Mighty whirlwind, I'm your master!
> Rescue us from this disaster,
> Now I give commandments three.
> Lift us! Drift us! Set us free!"

"Hey!" cried Magico-Porkus. "That's *my* spell. You *are* reading over my shoulder! That's not fair! Stop it at once!"

But he was too late. A sudden, fierce wind tossed the black cloud aside, then thrust itself through the open window. It flipped back the cover of Breeze's art project, and juggled with her bright drawings so that the air was filled with whirling art. Magico-Porkus was rocked to and fro, then toppled forwards on his snout, squealing with rage as he fell. The gold knob broke off his wand and rolled among the tin owls. One of the owls immediately hid the gold knob under its feathers. "We'll see what hatches out of *this*," Alpha heard it hooting. Then, as the fierce wind sucked its breath in, Alpha, Cathabelle and their three nameless sisters were swept off their round feet. They rose into the air, dancing and spiralling up, up, up like excited moths, and danced out through the window to where evening was snuggling softly down around the setting sun like a dark owl on a magical egg of gold.

"Terrifico!" cried Alpha. "Off on our adventures again."

"Oh dear," sighed Cathabelle. "I haven't had the chance to tell a single story."

"We *are* a story," Alpha said. "We're making it up as we go along, and, if we work at it, our story is bound to have a happy ending."

Chapter 7

Riding the Whirlwind

The wind that had whirled the five sisters away was not a summer breeze. It was a wild wind – a whirlwind – whistled out of nowhere by a wizard's spell. It tossed the five sisters head-over-heels across forty-two gardens. Then it whisked them past an underwear factory and a computer showroom, and tossed them higher than the highest building in the centre of the city. It roared like an angry genie, hurled them down to spin dizzily past fifteen floors filled with desks and computers, and then, just as they were about to be sucked among the cars that streamed endlessly through the city centre, it scooped them up again, twitching them, tugging them, and trying to tear them apart.

"What a powerful spell!" shouted Alpha. "But we'll be too strong for it as long as we hold on."

The five sisters were good at holding on. The wind stopped trying to tear them away from one another, and started tilting them *this* way, tilting them *that* way, first left, then right. Down below them they saw streets and traffic lights and car parks.

"Wheee!" shouted Alpha. "This is fun."

"I like it quieter," Cathabelle shouted back.

"Then why did you read the whirlwind spell with me?" Alpha asked, as they danced, jittering, past city windows.

"I didn't read any spell," Cathabelle said. "I couldn't see anything in that magician's book. My eyes are drawn looking to the left."

"Well, *someone* read it," Alpha said. "I felt the words of a spell flow into me. And we definitely said those words together."

"The spell came *through* me, not *from* me," said Cathabelle. "I think it came from the sister next to me. Remember, she has eyes now, but no mouth. She can see, but she can't speak. What are we going to do?"

But Alpha was looking out across the big city port, busy with tugs, container boats, cranes and front-end loaders. Beyond the port was the sea. Evening was all around them, and far, far away, on the distant horizon, Alpha saw her wonderful island once more, busy with bears and pirates and gallant explorers searching for lost cities.

"Look," she said to Cathabelle. "There's that island again. See the pirates burying treasure in the sand? It's an island of adventures."

"I can see the island," Cathabelle replied, "but I don't see the things you're seeing. I see a haunted house, and a tower with a handsome prince sound asleep in its very top room. Oh, there's a man made of gingerbread running along with a fox chasing after him. And there's a rabbit in a blue coat. It's an island of stories."

"Let's go there now," cried Alpha. "Follow me!"

"But we're falling," said Cathabelle. "Perhaps the spell is wearing out."

Cathabelle was right. Once again the sisters were fluttering towards the ground.

"We have been too strong for the wind, even though we are made of paper," muttered Alpha, smiling triumphantly, as they sank between two high-rise

buildings. The sea disappeared and, of course, the island
vanished too.

Wavering in the shifting air of the big city, the sisters
looked into lighted offices, then floated down past the
wide, bright windows of a big department store.

"Look at all those books," cried Cathabelle, staring into the window on the left side.

"Look at those ice-axes, kayaks and back-packs," cried Alpha, peering into the window on the right.

Then they both saw the city pavement. It was crowded with people, all hurrying backwards and forwards. The closer the sisters came to the ground the more dangerous it seemed to be.

"Look at those shoes! Look at those boots!" cried Cathabelle. "Our story is ending already. Why, within another second we're going to be trampled to bits."

Chapter 8

Sad Songs

A hand came swooping towards the sisters. It snatched them out of the air.

"Saved again!" cried Alpha happily.

"It doesn't quite feel like 'happy ever after' though," said Cathabelle.

The sisters were now being held by a young man called Simon.

"He's in love," Cathabelle whispered. Being a story-teller she could easily recognize things like that.

"Just our luck!" grumbled Alpha, for somehow she knew that love had ruined many promising adventures.

"He's trying to grow a moustache to make himself look older," Cathabelle went on. "And he plays the guitar and writes songs."

"Look what I've found," Simon said to his red-headed girlfriend, Marion. He waved the sisters at her.

"Where did you get *that*?" she asked scornfully.

"It was blowing in the wind," he replied. "Hey! That would be a good name for a song."

"Some kid must have thrown it away," said Marion. As she wasn't interested in the sisters, Simon really didn't want to be interested in them, either. However, he just couldn't help himself. "The first one is all scribbly, but the second one has been *painted*," he exclaimed, stopping under a street light to stare hard at Cathabelle. "She's been *carefully* painted," he said in astonishment. "And the third one has eyes, but no mouth."

A drop of water fell from the air on to the face of the third sister.

"It's going to *rain*," yelled Marion. "Don't stand there dreaming over rubbish! Chuck it away! I cleaned out my car this morning, and I don't want you filling it up with rubbish."

The rain began to fall more heavily. Marion scuttled for her car, and Simon hurried after her. As he hurried, he folded the sisters together, Alpha on top, and then pushed them all into the top pocket of his jacket. Alpha was able to look out over the rim of his pocket and see people putting up umbrellas or holding newspapers over their heads. Pictures of what she was seeing flowed down her arm and through her hand to the sisters folded under her.

"It's like a forest," she told them. "Not a forest of trees. Some sort of *city* forest." Yellow eyes lit up and glared at them. "Tigers," cried Alpha. But the yellow eyes were really headlights, for they were running through a car park, and it was raining hard. A moment later, Simon scrambled into the passenger seat of Marion's car, the five sisters still in his pocket.

"Hand in hand," sang Simon, pretending to strum a guitar, as Marion paid the car-park attendant. "Darkness behind and darkness before, we go hand in hand through the world's back door. Hey, that's not bad. Travelling on through a desolate land, we're strong as long as we're hand in hand. I seem to be getting a lot of hand-in-hand thoughts from somewhere."

He tried to hold Marion's hand.

"I'm driving," she cried. "I need both hands."

Marion drove through the city, and stopped by a big concrete warehouse. It was beginning to crumble at one end, but the windows at the other end were yellow with light.

"Come up for coffee?" asked Simon.

"Oh, Simon," said Marion. She sounded gentle for the first time that evening. "We mustn't go out together any more. We are just too different. You don't have a car, and I do. You don't have a job, and I do. If we go out anywhere I always have to pay for you, as well. And you actually *like* living in this old dump."

"I *have* to live in this old dump," Simon said. "I can't afford much rent. And I *do* work. I write songs."

"You and your songs! You don't get paid for them," said Marion. "Look, Simon, I really like you, but we're just too different." Simon got out of the car.

"OK! Goodnight," he said. "I'll ring you tomorrow."

"Don't ring," said Marion. "It will only make me cross, and I don't want to be cross. Let's just say goodbye and leave it at that." Then she drove away.

Later that night, when Simon undressed and threw his clothes on the floor, his jacket fell on the pile and Alpha, looking up from the pocket, was able to see there were tears in his eyes.

"He's raining," she whispered to Cathabelle, who was still folded under her.

Simon saw Alpha looking at him out of the top pocket of his jacket. He pulled her out, and unfolded her sisters from behind her. On the face of the third sister, just under her right eye with its long eyelashes, there was a curious blister where the raindrop had fallen on the paper. Simon picked up a black pen from the apple box beside his bed and drew a thin, broken line around the blister. It became a tear. He scribbled at her hair with the black pen until her hair was as black as night, but he left her hair ribbon white. Then he drew a round, blobby nose under her beautiful long-lashed eyes, and under the nose he drew her mouth. It was a smiling mouth, but the tear on her cheek made the smile a sad one.

"Sad! Sad! Sad!" Simon sang softly to himself as he drew. "*I'm feeling so mad. My baby has left me; the world's gone bad.*"

As he drew and sang, he had a strange feeling. He had always liked singing, but suddenly he felt the song swell up in him until he felt it take over his whole life. He felt that, no matter what else happened, he just *had* to be a singer for the rest of his life. Simon stopped his song and stared at the five sisters as if they had suddenly frightened him.

And then he shrugged his shoulders, crushed the fourth and fifth sisters, and tossed all five of them towards a big paper bag which stood gaping upwards behind the door. They fell straight into it.

"Bingo!" said Simon. "Good shot!"

He fell backwards on to his bed, and lay there, staring up at the ceiling.

"*Sad! Sad! Sad!*" he sang softly to himself once more. "*I'm feeling so mad. My baby has left me; the world's gone bad.*" And this time, as he sang, he accompanied himself on his invisible guitar.

Chapter 9

Throw-away Stuff

"Where are we now?" asked Alpha. "I can't see a thing."

"This paper bag counts as Simon's wastepaper basket," said a scrap of orange string. "Everything in here is going to be burnt sometime tomorrow."

"Tomorrow's Simon's cleaning day," said an empty envelope.

"Perhaps he'll forget," whispered a crumpled tissue. "He often forgets. His cleaning day only comes about once a year."

"Sooner or later we'll all be burnt though," said a piece of paper scribbled with lines, loops, arrows and crossed-out words. "We have to keep changing. I mean, look at me. I was part of a tree once. That tree had its roots deep in the world. Its roots drank the world's water and somehow they took in a lot of the world's secrets too. Then the tree was cut down and pulped and turned into

41

sheets of paper, but it took the secrets with it. That's one of the reasons paper has so many ideas hidden in it. It knows everything the tree once knew. Then the sheets of paper were glued together into a pad which Simon bought so that he could write his songs down. He began writing on the top sheet of the pad, and that top sheet was *me*. I did my best for him, but somehow he couldn't quite work out the words I was whispering to him. You know how most people have trouble hearing the voices of the world. Anyhow, he ripped me out of the pad, crumpled me up and tossed me right across the room into this bag. Bingo! I must say, though, he's a good shot."

"Is that what he's done with us?" asked Alpha. "Crumpled us up and thrown us away?"

"You bet he has," said a plastic bag. "We're all throw-away stuff in here."

"He might have heard the words I was secretly sing-ing, if only he'd worked on me a little bit longer," the thrown-away sheet of pad paper complained. "I can still feel that song struggling to break free from me. It wants to be heard. It wants to be sung."

"Wanting, but not wanted," said a new voice. Alpha and Cathabelle felt a curious thrill run through them.

"Who's that?" asked the piece of paper.

"Elodie," said the voice. "I'm the third sister, the one with the sad smile. The song's not wanted, and neither am I."

"Oh, yes you are," cried Alpha. "I want you."

"And so do I," agreed Cathabelle. "Are you the one that saved us with the whirlwind spell?"

"Yes," said Elodie. "Breeze painted my eyes so that

they looked straight ahead, and I could easily read that spell. But I couldn't *say* it because I didn't have a mouth back then. So I *thought* the words, and they ran along my arm and out through my right hand."

"They ran into *my* left hand, across my heart and out again," said Cathabelle.

"And they ran into me," said Alpha. "Cathabelle and I spoke together, magicked up the whirlwind, and wheeee! Off we went, dancing all the way."

"But there's no spell now," said Elodie. "We're going to be thrown on a fire tomorrow morning because we're not wanted."

"Hope for the best," said Alpha. "After all, Simon could have torn us to bits, but he didn't. Here we all are, still holding hands. Cheer up!"

"I can't," said Elodie. "I've been drawn with a tear on my cheek."

"Well, I will tell us a story or two," said Cathabelle. "That is what I can do. I can tell stories."

So, there in the wastepaper bag, Cathabelle began to tell stories about forests, dragons, lovers, and clever, talking animals. All the thrown-away stuff in the bag listened as well.

"Nothing's really lost," said Cathabelle at last. "It just changes. Everything changes. Cinderella changed, and so did Snow White. Stories should end by saying . . . *and they changed happily ever after*."

"Two of the three little pigs were lost," Elodie sighed. "The wolf ate them up."

"Yes," Cathabelle agreed, "but after a minute or two those little pigs began to be part of the wolf, and then they started understanding things from the wolf's point of view."

"We'll be part of the fire," said the bit of paper with the crossed-out song on it. "And we'll see things from the fire's point of view. Part of us will turn into heat and fly upward, and part of us will turn into ashes and they'll empty us around the lemon tree. So I suppose I'll change into soil and help beautiful yellow lemons to grow. I might even be part of those lemons."

"Changing! Changing!" the not-wanted stuff sang softly in the big paper bag.

"Being part of a garden might be a happy ending," said Cathabelle to Alpha and Elodie. "But I'd like to go on being Cathabelle for a little bit longer."

"I don't want to change either," Alpha said. "Not just yet! I want a lot of adventures first. More than anything, I

44

want to fly over the sea to that island on the edge of the sea."

"I think I'll be changed whether I want to be or not. I can't help shedding a tear," sighed Elodie.

Nor could she. She was drawn that way.

Next evening, Simon carried his big paper bag of rubbish out to an old oil drum at the bottom of the weedy garden. He emptied everything into the old oil drum, lit a match and held it to the unsuccessful song. Flames flickered a little, then leapt up and roared around the five sisters.

"Here I go!" cried the unsuccessful song, almost happily, as it blackened and broke. "Wish me luck!"

"Here we go!" Alpha, Cathabelle and Elodie cried too, and they *did* go, but not quite in the way they had expected and feared.

Chapter 10

Riding the Song

The five sisters did not catch fire, even though there were flames all around them. As the unsuccessful song blazed, it sang itself for the first and last time. It breathed out like a dragon, and the power of this great breath of heat and song and smoke not only set the air above the oil drum quivering, but sent big cinders spiralling upward. Pale and ghostly words could be seen, just for a second, on the frail, black cinders, before they crumbled away.

And the five sisters, still holding hands, flew upwards with the cinders and the song.

"Going my way?" said a familiar voice. It was yesterday's breeze. "Fancy meeting you again!"

"Rescue us!" shouted Alpha. "Carry us high."

"Oh, look," cried Elodie. "Is that the sea over there? Isn't it beautiful? And what's that little green land right on the edge of it?"

"That's the island I keep telling you about," said Alpha. "It seems to be following us around. Can you see the pirates?"

"Or the haunted house?" asked Cathabelle.

"I can't see any of those things," said Elodie. "I can see a quiet graveyard, and a shipwreck. I think some of the sailors must have been drowned because there are mermaids on the rocks and they are all weeping."

"Look, I'm not very strong today," the breeze complained. "There's a big space over there among the houses. I'll try to get you as far as that. Hold tight!"

"We will! We are!" cried Alpha.

"The story has rescued us," called Cathabelle. "It tossed us away from the fire."

"It was that song that lifted us free," Elodie reminded her. "A song about a broken heart."

"Well, songs and stories often run into one another," Cathabelle declared, holding on to Alpha who flew in front of them all.

Something ran like electricity from one hand to another.

"What can *that* be?" cried Alpha. "It's just as if someone tickled my thoughts. It feels – it feels like this . . ." And she made a strange sound as she flew – a sound she had never made before. "What does a sound like that mean?"

"You're laughing," said the breeze. "It doesn't have to mean anything much. It's just good fun. But I can't carry you any further. Laugh your way down to earth again."

And it let them go.

"More treetops," said Alpha. "Let's just flutter down through the leaves, and then we'll find out exactly where we are." But this time they did not flutter far. Alpha's round foot caught in a little tangle of twigs. Her fluttering stopped. Her four sisters drifted down past her. Alpha was held tightly, and, as she did her best to follow them, she slowly turned upside-down.

"Don't let go!" she called, and they didn't. They all ended by hanging upside-down among the leaves.

"Where are we going now?" asked Cathabelle.

"I don't know," confessed Alpha. "I think we might have to hang around here for a while."

Chapter 11

Hanging Around

The tree stood in a field of some kind. At one end of the field were long buildings with lots of windows, but they seemed to be dark and deserted.

"Where are we?" asked Cathabelle.

"Stuck in the top of a tree," said Alpha. "Hanging head downwards! I think it could get rather boring after an hour or two."

"But this tree is wonderful," said Elodie.

"Then why are you crying?" asked Alpha, puzzled.

"People can cry from happiness as well as sadness," Elodie explained.

"Will you be quiet!" chirped a bird sitting on a nest one branch below them. "I don't want you waking my eggs until they're really ready to hatch. What are you doing here, anyway?"

"Just hanging around," said Alpha. "We'll be moving

on as soon as I can get my foot free. Can you tell us where we are?"

"In my tree," said the bird.

"Yes," said Cathabelle. "But where is the tree?"

"Everywhere, really," said the bird. "Its top is in the air, its roots are in the ground, and the rest of it is in between."

"Who lives in that large house over there?" asked Elodie.

"That's not a house," squawked the bird scornfully. "That's a school. St Ronan's Utterly Intelligent High School. Something like that, anyway."

"A school?" asked Alpha. "What happens at a school?"

"I don't know," the bird exclaimed. "Children without feathers thump in and out nearly every day. But they never seem to learn anything useful. None of them can fly."

"Let's move on," said Alpha. But though she tried and tried, she couldn't pull her foot free from the twigs. The five sisters had to hang around. Looking up through the leaves, they could see the sky, peppered all over with grains of light.

"We're seeing stars," said Elodie. "Even if it is a sad world, it is a beautiful one."

"I wouldn't mind shooting out between the stars in a space ship," said Alpha. "That would be an adventurous thing to do."

"There are lots of stories with stars in them," said Cathabelle, and told one or two. The bird had its head under its wing, but every now and then it opened one eye which shone in the darkness. Cathabelle knew it was listening.

The stars moved across the sky. Then, at last, a line of pale light began to stretch itself along the eastern edge of the city. The line turned into a pink stain, spreading up through the air as the stars sank down. The bird on the nest woke up as her husband, along with a lot of other birds, began to sing. Slowly the whole sky turned pink and, in the east, the city seemed to burn with gold.

"What's happening?" asked Cathabelle. "Is the city burning up? Will we see cinders with ghostly words on them flying past us and crumbling away? Poems falling apart?"

"There's no smoke," said Alpha.

"A burning edge has pushed up into the sky," said Elodie. "It's the sun. It must be morning."

She wept with happiness to see the sun. As she wept, that strange feeling, like the ghost of a laugh, swept from one to the other of them once more.

People began moving around in the streets. Birds began hopping around on the grass, searching for worms. More and more cars and trucks roared down the motorway. Inside the school someone turned on lights.

"Where *is* that breeze?" asked Alpha impatiently. "Or even the whirlwind! I'm sick of hanging around."

People started to come through the school gate and walk under the tree.

"Time for me to stretch my wings," said the bird. It hopped off its nest and on to a twig.

"Once around the playground, then back again," it said. "See you soon!" And off it flew. Its wings made a little bird-breeze which was just strong enough to push Alpha's foot free from the trap of twigs.

"At last! At last!" she shouted. "Follow me!"

Her sisters had to follow her whether they wanted to or not. Holding hands they dived down through the branches, and as they dived they heard a bell begin to ring.

There was no wind to carry the five sisters across the school grounds.

"Where are we going?" asked Cathabelle and Elodie together.

"Who cares?" Alpha replied. "We're going *somewhere*. That's all that matters."

"You are going to your doom," said a leaf as it fluttered by. "You are going *down*. Your autumn has come."

The sisters fell to churned and muddy ground beside a path. They lay there helplessly, while big feet ran and leapt and trampled all around them. At last, one particular foot in a huge sports shoe rose right over them. The sole blotted out the sun. It hid the sky. The pattern on the sole looked like an eclipsing black labyrinth falling down on them, determined to crush them into the mud so ruthlessly they would never rise again.

Chapter 12

Chemistry

But the foot changed direction in mid-air. It quivered, skipped over the sisters, skidded a little, then stopped. It stepped carefully back again. Four fingers and a thumb swooped down and snatched the sisters up into the air again.

"Hey, look what came tumbling out of that tree," said the boy whose name was Craig.

"Paper dolls don't fall out of trees," said his friend, Don, scornfully. "Some little kid must have dropped them."

"I *saw* them falling when we were back by the gate. I thought it was a weird sort of butterfly," said Craig. "Look! One red scribbly one! One painted in lots of colours! One with black eyes and a tear . . ."

"Aw, come *on*!" shouted Don. "Are you going to muck around with paper dolls all day? First bell's gone. We'll get a rocket from Dr Dracula if we're late."

Craig folded up the sisters. Then he pushed them between the pages of a fat book which stuck out of the canvas pack he was carrying across one shoulder.

"We're in prison," cried Alpha.

"We're in a book," said Cathabelle, "but it's not a story-book. What are these little black things crawling all over the pages like ants?"

"Numbers! We're numbers!" said the small signs printed on the pages. They chuckled to one another. "We're a secret language."

Craig forgot about the sisters who had fluttered down so magically from the tree until later in the morning when his teacher – the one he and Don called Dr Dracula – told the class to open their books at page 25. Craig opened his book, and there, at page 25, the sisters were waiting for him.

He couldn't help being interested in them. Alpha looked so adventurous, Cathabelle was beautifully painted, and Elodie's sad smile seemed to have mystery in it. Craig looked at each of them in turn, and then at the two crumpled, faceless sisters at the end of the line. He propped his big book in front of him so Dr Dracula couldn't see what he was doing behind it.

He drew a long blue nose on the fourth sister. Then he snapped his pen, which could write in ten different colours, to black, and drew round black eyes looking upwards under spiky lashes as if they were studying the stars. Next, he drew straight eyebrows, and then, snapping the pen to scarlet, he added a wide, clever smile. Eyes, nose, clever smile . . . the face of the fourth sister seemed to have everything a face needed. All the same, Craig frowned. A crease like a scar ran from her right

cheek across the bridge of her nose and up to her left eyebrow. He couldn't smooth that crease away, but, as he frowned over it, Craig thought of a way to hide it. He drew double scarlet circles around the black eyes and joined them together with a scarlet line, following the crease across the top of the long nose. This sister was wearing red glasses, a sign that she was a deep thinker.

As Craig drew the glasses he felt himself changing.

He had always enjoyed maths and science, but suddenly he began to feel that science was not just something that he had to learn at school because his teacher told him to. It was as if he really wanted to know for himself exactly how the world hung together. He seemed to hear voices saying, "Hold on! Don't let go!" and he knew at once that, though he wasn't going to hear them very often, the world was full of secret voices like these. "What are they all saying?" he wondered. "These sisters are putting a spell on me."

Then a voice said his name, but this time it was a voice he recognized at once.

"Craig, you seem very busy behind that book," said Dr Dracula, showing his fangs in a sarcastic smile. "Perhaps you'd like to explain the next step to the class." Craig hastily slid the sisters between the pages of his book. Strange, scientific words, rather like a spell from the book of Magico-Porkus, came bursting into his mind.

"Covalent bonding . . ." he began. Though he could hear his voice saying these words, Craig knew that someone was secretly telling him what to say. Dr Dracula was amazed at his good answer. Craig sat down, a little frightened, and shut the sisters into the book at page 27.

"I hate this," said Alpha. "All the pages in front of us are crushing in on me."

"Those numbers tell a different sort of story from the stories I tell," murmured Cathabelle.

"Life is heavy and dark sometimes," sighed Elodie. "It is difficult to understand."

"But isn't it interesting? Aren't you excited?" cried a new voice. "I'll explain it to you, and then you'll be excited and interested, too."

"Who's that?" asked Alpha. "Who's talking?"

"Me," said the new voice. "Icasia – fourth one along."

"One, two, three, four!" called numbers printed on the page of the book. "You can count on us!"

"Another sister has found a voice," shouted Alpha. "Hooray!"

"Wonderful!" exclaimed Cathabelle.

"Welcome!" sighed Elodie, weeping with joy.

"It's marvellous to have a voice at last," said Icasia. "I know you sisters have talked and looked at the world for me, but it's always best to talk and see for yourself."

"Do you want to wander?" asked Alpha.

"Or tell stories?" suggested Cathabelle.

"Or weep?" sobbed Elodie.

"I want to find out," said Icasia. "That's why I don't mind being shut up in this book. It's a book written to explain the world – a chemistry book. And we've got useful work to do at last. We're a bookmark."

Chapter 13

Bookmark Life

So the five sisters began their bookmark life in between the pages of a chemistry book. They weren't always at the same page of course. Craig kept moving them. In the darkness of the shut book, Icasia told her sisters everything on each page they found themselves marking.

"Covalent bonding," read Icasia. "A chemical bond formed by two atoms sharing a pair of electrons," she repeated.

"What's that?" asked Alpha. It all sounded like nonsense to her.

"It's one of the ways the world holds itself together," Icasia explained. "It's like us, holding hands and never letting go."

"If we don't hold hands we wouldn't be us," Elodie said.

"Without covalent bonding the world wouldn't be the world," Icasia replied. "Books, trees, birds, buildings,

pages of paper . . . deep inside them the world is holding hands with itself."

A few days later Craig had to sit a chemistry exam. He
worked quite hard for it because he had suddenly be-
come interested in chemistry, but he couldn't help feeling a bit nervous as he bent over the exam paper. He
need not have worried. All the way through the exam he
thought he could hear a voice coming from nowhere,
gossiping about covalent bonding and other useful
things just when he most needed to know about them.
He thought it might be the voice of his memory, but
really it was Icasia explaining the book to her sisters.

Alpha would have yawned, if she had been drawn
that way. She was the first sister, the leader, the

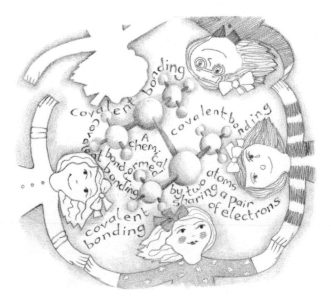

adventurer. She wanted to be up and doing. But a bookmark has to stay still, guarding a place . . . marking a page. Craig had moved her to page 57 by now, but from Alpha's point of view, one part of the book was very like another.

"Energy," read Icasia, a few weeks later. "The world is the dancer, and energy is the name of the dance." She whispered the words into Craig's head as he bent over a school test.

"But we're not dancing, we're standing still," complained Cathabelle.

"The dance is still going on inside us," said Icasia. "The paper we're made of is dancing. It only *seems* to be standing still. We *are* the dance."

"I wish I could dance," Alpha mumbled to herself. "I want to dance all the way across the sea to that island and dig up the treasure the pirates were burying in the sand. I could swing from creepers and fight with swords, and here I am doing a full-time job as a bookmark."

"I want to climb the tower and kiss the sleeping prince," said Cathabelle. "I know that island is just bursting with stories."

"I'd love to visit that island too," sighed Elodie. "Being a bookmark is such dark, *heavy* work, what with all those pages pressing down on us."

But they had to go on doing bookmark work for weeks and months, helping Craig remember what was in the book, particularly when he was being tested on what he knew, and was not allowed to open it. And then school was over for the summer.

"Hooray! No more chemistry until after the holidays," cried Craig.

"Hooray! Bookmark days are over," cried Alpha, but this time Craig did not hear her. He pushed his book on to a dark shelf in a dark corner of his room, and forgot all about it. Other books were read and replaced, but that particular chemistry book was not chosen any more. Craig had new books about the dance in the heart of everything. The five sisters had to stay clamped between pages 200 and 201.

"Once upon a time there were two sisters called Snow White and Rose Red," began Cathabelle, telling a story to pass the time.

"Every colour in the world is somehow hidden in the colour white," said Icasia. The two voices ran into one another. It was like hearing two people tell the same story at the same time, but in two different voices and from two different points of view.

"I might as well listen," thought Alpha. "It looks as if I'll never ever reach that island."

Then, one day, a hand (not Craig's) took the book down, banged the cover to send the dust flying out of it, and packed it into a box with a lot of other books. The lid came down on the box, and the sisters were shut in a darkness darker than any other darkness they had ever encountered before. No one opened the book. And of course there were no city lights inside the book. There were no stars, and certainly no shining island beckoning from the edge of the sea.

"It feels like the end of a story," exclaimed Cathabelle.

"Perhaps it is *our* end," whispered Elodie. "After all, everything ends, sooner or later."

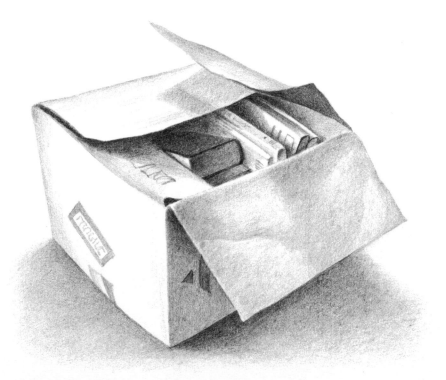

"Everything *changes*," Icasia corrected her. "We might have to wait a while, but, sooner or later, we will change too."

The old books murmured to each other, cover to cover in the darkness.

"Once upon a time . . ." "Then *this* happened!" "Then *that* happened!" "Suddenly, out of the jungle . . ." ". . . and they lived happily ever after. The end!" they whispered.

Alpha yawned.

"Well, if there are no adventures, I might have a little nap," she said.

"Me too," said Cathabelle. "I might dream. Dreams are like stories."

"I'd love some beautiful dreams," said Elodie, "though they'd probably make me cry in my sleep."

"I've described the dance," said Icasia. "So now I'll hibernate. That means I'll be in a dormant state," she added, explaining the world as she always did. "I'll wake up when we're put into some other book, and I can begin my finding-out again."

Alpha could not close her eyes, but she found she could sleep with them open. "I'll wake up when I need to," she thought. Then, just before she began her nap, she felt for the second time that very strange feeling running from Cathabelle's hand into hers. It tickled.

"What is it?" Alpha asked.

"Laughing," said Cathabelle. "Someone is laughing. But it isn't me. I'm too sleepy, and anyway, I don't think there's anything to laugh about."

And then the five sisters all fell asleep for what turned out to be a long, long time.

Chapter 14

Press Lightly

Light burst in on them. It was like another sunrise. Someone had opened the dusty box, and had then opened the old book.

"Mum," cried a voice . . . a small voice. "Look what I've found. Five little girls."

"Let me see," said another, older voice . . . a light, kind one. Then it cried, "Good heavens! Where did you get this?" The older voice suddenly sounded so excited it was almost as if it were frightened.

"I know that voice," thought Alpha dreamily. She squeezed Cathabelle's hand as the sticking-out ears under her scribbly hair began listening in to the world once more.

"Who kissed us awake?" asked Cathabelle drowsily. "How long have we been sleeping?"

"That kind voice does remind me of another voice,"

said Elodie, "but it was a long time ago, and it's not quite my own memory. Whose memory is it?"

"I think it's mine," said Alpha, "because that is the very first voice I ever heard."

"Craig! Craig!" called the very first voice Alpha had ever heard. "Come and see what Olivia's found. Where did you find it, Livy?"

"Shut in one of those old books," said the smaller voice.

"Be gentle with them – very gentle," said the familiar voice. "They're so old, so frail, they might fall to pieces. Give them to me."

The sisters slid into kind hands.

"Nana once drew them for *me*," said the woman who was now holding them. It truly was Sally. Sally grown up now, and with a child of her own. "It was right here by the lily pond, one hot, still day," she told her

daughter Olivia, who had been unpacking a box of old dusty books. "Nana folded the paper, drew this wild, scribbly, red girl and then cut her out so carefully. I was going to draw faces on all the other sisters, but then they disappeared. I searched and searched but I couldn't find them. I was so disappointed. Nana told me to forget them, but I said I would never forget, and you see I *didn't* forget. I have remembered them clearly over all these years."

A man came into the shed. It was Craig, grown up too.

"How's the big clean-up going?" he asked. "Find any treasures in those old boxes?"

"Yes," said Sally. "But it's my treasure, not yours." She held out the sisters towards him. "Look what Livy found, shut in one of your old books? Where on earth did you find *this*?"

"Good heavens! That's my good-luck bookmark," Craig said. "It sounds crazy but that cut-out came fluttering down out of a tree on the day before a chemistry exam. I used them for a bookmark, and they brought me luck. I came top of the class for the first time in my life."

"The wind must have blown the sisters all the way across the city," said Sally. "How funny! You know, in those days I thought I'd be a great traveller. I even used to imagine there was an island in the harbour, on the very edge of the sea, and that I would sail there one day and live on the beach like Robinson Crusoe. However, it's this little red, scribbly girl who has done all the travelling, not me."

"Well, you travelled just as far as she did – from one side of the city to the other," said Craig, pulling his arm around her. "We wouldn't have met, otherwise."

"Going across the city must have been like going around the world to the scribbly girl," said Olivia. "What do the other sisters look like?"

"Oh, none of the other girls have faces," said Sally. "They vanished before I had time to draw them."

"Well, you're wrong there," said Craig. "Look!" He took the sisters from Sally's hand, and unfolded them very carefully. Little scales of paper flaked from around their cracking, brittle edges, but the sisters still held hands tightly and stayed together, even though they were now so delicate.

"I drew that one," Craig said, pointing to Icasia. "Doesn't she look clever?"

"But who drew the others?" asked Olivia, staring at Cathabelle and Elodie.

Craig shrugged.

"They were like that when I found them," he said. "Someone has painted the second one quite carefully."

69

He looked at Cathabelle, half smiling and half frowning. "In fact, it reminds me of those pictures by that famous artist, Breeze Someone-or-other."

"She'd be worth a fortune then," said Sally, laughing. "Breeze Grafton's pictures sell for thousands of dollars these days, particularly the ones of owls and magical pigs. But Breeze Grafton's pictures are great art, and this is just playing."

"Great art is a sort of playing," Alpha found herself thinking. But these words weren't *her* words. They ran up her arm, and were followed by that *thrill* she could not explain, even though she had felt it twice before.

"Was that you?" she asked Cathabelle.

"No!" said Cathabelle. "It came to my hand from Elodie."

"It came to me from Icasia," said Elodie.

"I didn't invent it," Icasia murmured. "It came to me from the sister without a face. The one like the map of all our travels."

"I'm going to draw a face on the last sister," cried Olivia, just as if she had heard what the sisters had been saying to one another. "She's been waiting for a long time. Now, she must have a face too."

"Be very careful," said Sally. "Press lightly. Look, the paper's split and creased and wrinkly. I think she must have got wet somewhere in her travels."

Chapter 15

Finished at Last

Olivia took the five sisters to her room, and spread them out on a desk which had once been Sally's . . . Alpha, Cathabelle, Elodie, Icasia and the faceless, nameless sister who was going to be given a face and a name at last.

Using her pastels, Olivia coloured her in with soft, quick strokes – a pink dress, a pink hair ribbon and pink cheeks. The scratches, splits and wrinkles showed through, but Olivia knew she must press lightly, and the fifth sister did not fall to pieces. As she worked delicately Olivia felt something happening to her. She had always liked laughing, but suddenly she felt laughter swell up in her until she felt it was going to live in her for ever. It was not just that the world was funny, but that it was so astonishing. Olivia laughed aloud from the surprise and happiness of being alive. She stopped laughing and stared at the five sisters as if they had suddenly frightened her. But then she laughed again and gave the fifth sister brown eyes and yellow frizzy hair. But she could not hide the lines beneath, so that in the end the fifth sister looked like a ghost haunted by another ghost . . . the ghost of a map.

At last, Olivia picked up the red pastel.

"A smiling mouth," she thought to herself. "A big, wide smile."

Something ran like electricity up the red pastel and along her arm.

"What's that?" she wondered, rubbing her elbow. "Something *joggled* me, just when I was trying to be careful."

She looked at the face she had drawn. The line of the smile began as one line, then split in two, running along either side of a crease (which Simon had made when he crumpled the fifth sister), and *then* joined up with itself again.

"I've drawn her laughing," Olivia cried in amazement. "I meant to draw a smile but I've drawn a laugh, by accident."

She stood the five sisters in a zigzag row.

"Zamira!" said the fifth sister. Her voice was so small and mysterious that Olivia did not really hear it. Nevertheless the name flew into her ear like a dancing gnat, and – zzzz!

"Zzzamira," said Olivia doubtfully. She liked the sound of the name, and smiled.

"Zamira!" she said again, loving the sound this time.

"Welcome! Welcome!" cried Alpha, Cathabelle, Elodie and Icasia. "We can have adventures. We can tell stories. We can cry. We can learn. We can laugh! Finished at last! Finished at last!"

Olivia's brother Yeats came bouncing past her bedroom door.

"I'm going down to the beach," he shouted. "Coming?"

"Look what I've found!" said Olivia. "Five sisters. They're very old. Mummy's Nana cut them out for Mummy when Mummy was a little girl, and then they got lost. I think they must have blown away across town, because they fell out of a tree at Daddy's school, and they brought him luck in his exam. Anyhow, there they were, shut in one of his old books."

"Are *you* going to use them as a bookmark?" asked Yeats, picking them up gingerly. Alpha's skirt crackled a little at the edge.

"No," shouted Alpha. "No more bookmark life. We want adventures."

"Stories," called Cathabelle.

73

"Beauty," cried Elodie.

"Knowledge," muttered Icasia.

"Jokes," laughed Zamira.

Their voices were like a lot of world voices, too small to be heard, but somehow or other Yeats and Olivia seemed to understand them.

"Let's take them down to the beach," said Yeats. "Look what I've made."

He had folded a boat out of a single sheet of newspaper.

"They could go sailing at the edge of the sea. This ship needs a crew."

"Hooray!" shouted Alpha.

Olivia looked interested.

"The sea's adventurous," she said. "There are lots of stories about the sea. And it's beautiful, too. I think they'd like it." Cathabelle and Elodie nodded.

"You can tell the sea thinks a lot by the way it wrinkles its forehead," whispered Icasia. "The sea is OK by me."

"It chuckles on sand, and giggles in and out of the rocks," Zamira agreed. "It's got a good sense of humour. Let's go to the sea!"

"The sea! The sea!" called the five sisters. "Let's go to the sea."

"Let's go to the sea," said Olivia. She thought that going to the sea was all her own idea, but then she stopped and frowned. "Did you hear someone calling and laughing?"

"It was someone a long way off," Yeats said.

As they went through the sitting room the radio was playing a sad song. Sally and Craig were dancing together, and laughing as they danced. Their children looked at them in surprise.

"They're playing our tune," Craig called. "This is a Simon Payne song. We always liked dancing to his songs in the old days."

"He was born in this city," said Sally. "He was married three times and made a million dollars singing sad songs about broken hearts."

"What a drongo!" mumbled Yeats.

"Some people *like* feeling sad," Elodie whispered. "You can be happy in sadness."

"You can laugh out of sorrow," said Zamira, "another one of the world's jokes."

Chapter 16

Yo ho!

As they came down to the edge of the sea, Yeats and Olivia heard the voices of baby kingfishers churring and peeping in the holes in the bank. The parent kingfishers sat in the tree watching Yeats put his paper boat into the water. A wave swept it in towards the sand, then carried it back again.

"The sea air will do you good," Olivia told the five sisters. "There's almost no wind at all. You'll be perfectly safe."

"Nothing's ever quite perfect," said Icasia.

"Nothing's ever quite safe," added Alpha. "And even if it was, it's better to be an adventurer and crumble around the edges, than a perfectly safe bookmark. Blow hard, all of you, blow hard! We'll be our own breeze this time round."

All five sisters blew hard. The sea foam shivered a little. The wave that had flung itself on the sand rushed back, and then, before Yeats and Olivia could quite stop it, the paper boat had somehow slipped back on to another, bigger wave which pulled it further out to sea.

"They're floating away from us," shouted Olivia. "Stop them! Stop them!"

Yeats ran into the water with a stick. He was just about to hook the stick over the edge of his paper boat and pull it back to shore again, when a little breeze came sneaking out over the water.

"Oh, hello!" it said. "You lot again!"

"Are you the same breeze that let us fall in front of the lawn-mower?" asked Alpha.

"Are you the same breeze that dropped us into the tree in the school yard?" asked Elodie.

"We breezes get around," said the breeze. "Remember, I *did* pick you up when you were tossed up out of the fire. Do you really want those kids to rescue you?"

"No, no!" Alpha cried. "We want to be blown to the island on the edge of the sea."

Yeats had hooked the end of his stick over the edge of his paper boat, but the breeze rocked it out from under the stick, and then pushed it two waves back, where Yeats could not reach it.

"I'm sailing! I'm really sailing," the paper boat shouted, sweeping up one side of a much bigger wave and down the other. "I'm a real ship now, not a mere paper nothing. I'm at sea with my gallant crew. Yo ho!"

"We'll all have salty tales to tell," said Cathabelle, nodding wisely.

"It's like sailing through tears," said Elodie. "Happy ones!"

"Common salt. Sodium chloride," Icasia told her sisters in scientific language. "Sharing electrons holds the sodium and the chlorine together, and makes salt strong."

"We're five strong old salts," cried Zamira, laughing. "Salt of the earth. Yo ho ho! And what's that on the edge of the sea?"

"There it is at last! The island of pirates and buried treasure," cried Alpha.

"The island of forests and fairy tales," said Cathabelle.

"The island in the middle of the sea of tears," said Elodie.

"The island of holding on and letting go," said Icasia.

Zamira laughed.

"Oh yes! I see it clearly now," she said. "It's the island

where all good jokes begin before they fly off into the world. You know, once we get there, we might . . . we just *might* . . . be able to stop holding hands for a while. It might be nice to go in different directions for a little bit – as long as we come back together afterwards, that is, and hold hands again.''

"We'll always do that," said Alpha. "Off we go. Yo ho ho!"

The little boat sailed through the deep sea, washing from wave to wave. The sun set and left the new moon flying through the sky like a silver bird – perhaps an owl – hatched out of an egg of gold.

The voices of the world sang and whispered and grumbled and joked and argued all around them, and they bobbed towards their mysterious island . . . five sisters, all with names and faces, all with smiles, all holding hands, and all free at last.